Wacky Quack 2

Dedication

Preston Gray Chellew

This is a Book 1 (See last page for parents and Book grades)

The Beginning

In the beginning, God created all the ducks – White ones, brown ones, multi-coloured ones – all sorts of colours.

Wacky Quack was born at Beulah, Paeroa – right in the

middle of everywhere in New
Zealand.
It was a land of milk and honey
for ducks of every kind.

Beulah had everything that
ducks and geese liked.

It had green grasslands,

stream and ponds, and even

generous quantities of grain-

food – the sort that ducks

loved.

Wacky Quack was a real
greedy duck.

Just like his friend Wonky Honkey

They fought for their food.

He quickly learned that the white ducks were very noisy and would not come too close to Pakehas.

And not at all like his good
friend Wonky Honkey.

Wonky only had ONE leg.

The other was bitten off by Evil Knievel – an Eel that lives in the Beulah pond.

Birds can sing songs!

Just like parrots – see the
Youtube that went viral.

YouTube

My Sunshine

My Sunshine is 76 years old today.

Beulah Stories

Behind
The Pictures

YOU ARE
MY
SUNSHINE

MY ONLY SUNSHINE
YOU MAKE
ME HAPPY

WHEN SKIES
ARE GRAY

YOU'LL NEVER KNOW

DEAR HOW MUCH
I LOVE YOU

Dee and Preller Geldenhuys

Sing my favourite song!

You are my Sunshine,

my only sunshine

You make my happy
When skies are grey

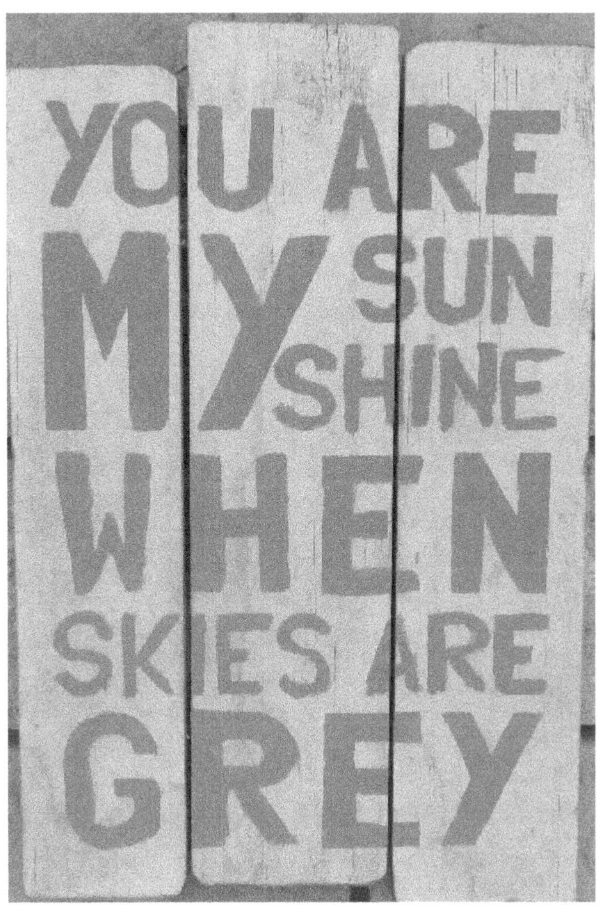

You never know, dear.

How much I love you.

So please do not take my
Sunshine Away.

(Sung to Gogga at 2:20am on
her birthday)

You are my
Sunshine
my only sunshine
you make me happy
when skies are grey
you'll never know, dear, how much
I LOVE YOU
Please don't take my sunshine away.

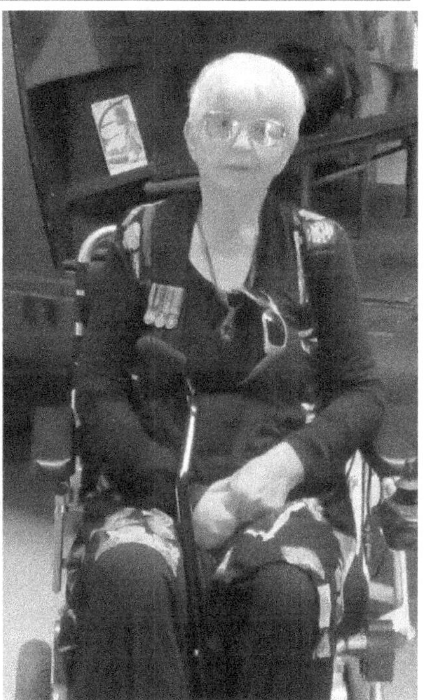

you are my
SUNSHINE
my only sunshine
you make me
HAPPY
when skies are gray
you'll never know
dear how much
I LOVE YOU
please don't take
my sunshine away

19

Difficulty

I can spell 'difficulty' –

Mr D, Mr I, Mr FFI,

Mr C, Mr U, Mr LTY

= D I FF I C U LT Y

Acknowledgements

Preston Grey Chellew
deserves the best opportunity
to read and write, do arithmetic
and master calculus.

Oumie (Nana) for line
drawings.

Wonky Honky -
https://www.amazon.com/dp/B08X
P9JTYR

Beulah Series –

Beulah Places -
https://www.amazon.com/dp/B08L
1QD8SW

Other Books

Little Red Riding Hood

Based on the story by The Brothers Grimm
Illustrated by Mike Gordon

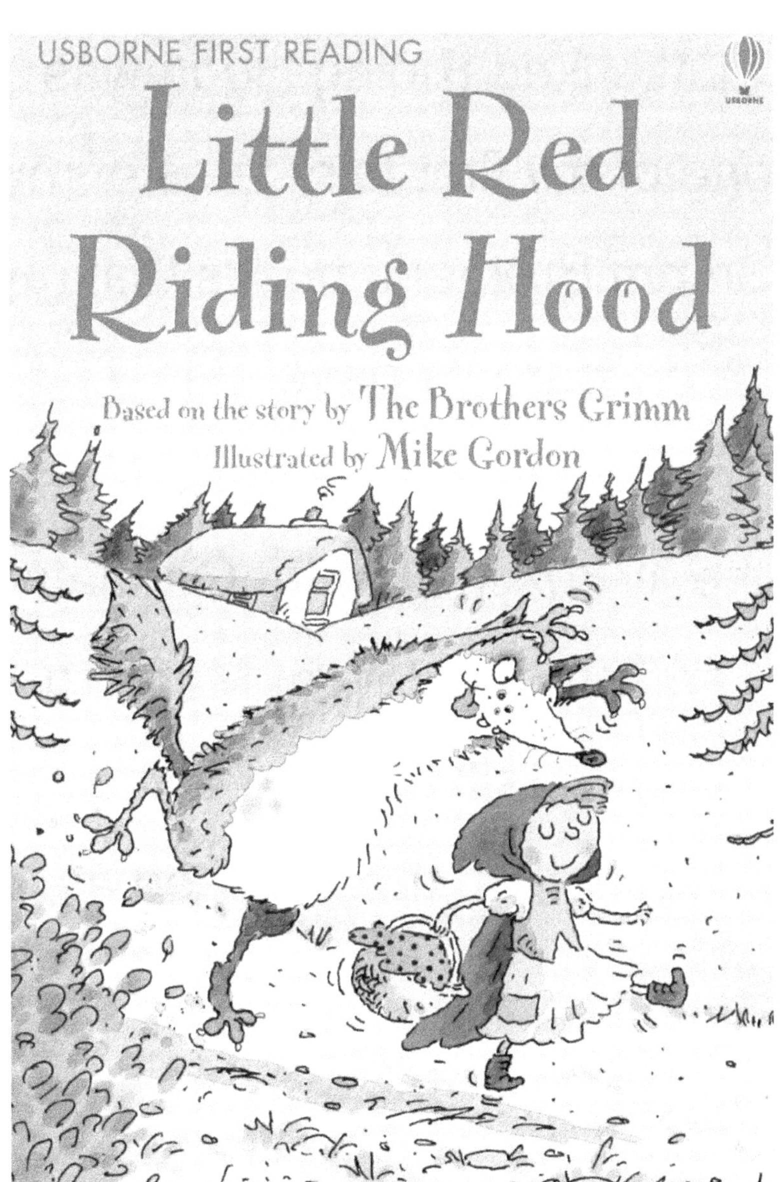

Little Red Riding Hood was one of my first fairy tales of my Grimm Brother's books that my parents gave me.

The brothers were born during the 1780s in Hanau, Germany and studied law at Marburg University. After leaving education, they worked as

diplomats and librarians in
Kassel.

In 1837 they were dismissed
from their professorships at the
University of Göttingen for
refusing to swear allegiance to
the new King of Hanover but
were later invited to join the
Academy in Berlin, by
Frederick William IV of Prussia.

They remained there for the rest of their lives. Individually and as a team the brothers were two of the great scholars that Germany has produced. Wilhelm died in 1859 at age 73 and Jacob died in 1863 at age 78.

Grimms'
Fairy Tales

J.L.C. & W.C. GRIMM

USBORNE FIRST READING
Goldilocks
and the
Three Bears
Bear Cottage
Retold by
Susanna Davidson
Illustrated by Mike Gordon

Goldilocks and the Three Bears

Retold by Susanna Davidson
Narrated by Lesley Sims

Illustrated by Mike Gordon

Reading Consultant: Alison Kelly

The Hare and the Tortoise

Retold by
Mairi Mackinnon

Illustrated by
Daniel Howarth

The Story of
Black Beauty
with
AUDIO
Illustrated by
Alan Marks

Animal Fairy Tales
Cat and the
Beanstalk
written by Charlotte Guillain & Illustrated by Dawn Beacon

Jack and the Beanstalk

Cinderella

Snow White (and the seven dwarfs)

Hansel and Gretel

Sleeping Beauty

Aladdin and the Lamp

Rapunzel

Rapunzel is the Grimm brothers fairy tale of a witch who imprisons a baby girl in a tall tower. The girl grows golden locks which she lets down to the witch, who then climbs up to bring Rapunzel food. A handsome Prince hears singing whilst riding his horse deep into the forest one day. He notices the witch climb up Rapunzel's hair – and does the same.

The Prince plans to rescue Rapunzel but the witch tricks the Prince. He falls and is blinded. Rapunzel throws the witch out the window, climbs down the rope of hair, kisses the prince whose sight is restored and they galop off to his castle where they marry and live happy ever after.

I Love My Dog
by
Angela Smith
PROUD SUPPORTER
PAW JUSTICE

i LOVe You BooK
by
Libby Hathorn
Illustrated by
Heath McKenzie

"My hope is that Wonky's strong spirit will inspire people of all ages to believe in themselves, no matter what life brings"
Lazy Daisy, Busy Lizzie
Mary Ellen Jordan & Andrew Welden
PDF

Lazy Daisy, Busy Lizzie
Mary Ellen Jordan
& Andrew Welden

40

Little Red Riding Hood

Once upon a time there was a kind little girl called Little Red Riding Hood.

She always wore a bright red cloak with a bright red hood.

The map of the deep dark woods where the grandmother lived.

Little Red Riding Hood lived with her mother on the edge of some deep, dark woods.

The wolf knocked on the door.

"Let yourself in" said the
grandmother.

The wolf leaped into the room.

He gobbled up Little Red
Riding Hood's grandmother.

He then climbed into bed to
wait for Little Red Riding Hood.

"I've brought you some vegetable soup," said Little Red Riding Hood.

"Lovely," snarled the wolf. "I mean *lovely*!" he added in a squeak.

"Put the basket on the stool and come and sit next to me."

Little Red Riding Hood looked

at her grandmother.

She looked again.

"All the better to hug you with,"

said the wolf.

Little Red Riding Hood was now standing right next to the bed.

And the grandmother sewed
the tummy up.

Peppa Pig Stories

Mouse and Peppa pig

Pig and Kitty Cat

Peppa's summer holiday to the coast.

The family travel to the airport

They showed their passports
and tickets.

The air hostess showed them
to their seats.

Daddy saw the sea; Mummy pig noticed the palm trees but Peppa pig liked the swimming pool.

Daddy Pig jumped into the pool.

Miss Rabbit arrived at the pool
made an announcement.
"Attention please! This afternoon's holiday
is a visit to a turtle sanctuary."
"Oooh!" gasped the children.
"If turtle hatchlings are being released into
the sea today, we may be able to watch them
from a distance!" said Miss Rabbit.

Peppa pig meets her friends.

They ask Mummy to go to the pool.

Splash! Splash!

The next day, Peppa and George went straight to the pool.
"Suzy! Zoe!" cried Peppa. "What are you doing here?"
"We're on holiday!" replied Suzy Sheep and Zoe Zebra.

Hee!
Hee!
Hee!
Hee!

It was very hot in the jungle.
"Please can we go back to the swimming pool now, Mummy?" said Peppa.
"Of course," replied Mummy Pig. "It'll be nice to cool off in the pool."

It was hot in the jungle.

Peppa wanted one last swim.

Peppa pig sits in front of his mother.

Her brother sits in front of his father.

Every one loved their holiday.

George enjoys swimming too!

George enjoys swimming!

Adult advice

Encourage your children to
read books.

Take them to your local library
at soon as possible – to
choose their own books - to
read at their leisure.

Book Grading

 Ideal for sharing with emergent readers

 Simple sentences for eager new readers

 High-interest stories for developing readers

 Complex plots for confident readers

 The perfect bridge to chapter books

**For more information about the
I Can Read Book® series, see inside!**

1 = Yellow + Blue – Babies

2 = Red - Age 3 to 5 years

3 = Green – complex plots

4 = Purple – Chapter books

Cover design: Peysoft Publishing

ISBN: 979-874379383-9
And: 979-873286443-4
ePub: (TBA)

Other books in this Series: -
Wonky Honkey
Wacky Quack
Wacky Quack 2
Two Tongue
Red Riding Hood
Peppa Pig